MY UPS AND DOWNS

via

POETRY

BY:

SAM BARDER

CONTENTS

Where Is Love

In the warmth of someone's eyes,
    The humor from their heart;
In the caring about little things,
    Before the big things start.

In the closeness of a dance,
    As if no one else were around;
In the waiting for the chance,
    To prove this love is sound.

In the fragile veil placed about you,
    To keep you happy as a lark;
Not confining or overbearing,
    So as not to stifle your spark.

In the shared kindness and respect,
    That everyone desires;
These are the kindling and the logs,
    That add warmth to the fire.

In the leading, by the hand,
    Instead of nudging from behind;
And sometimes the tear,
        that comes to the eye,
When you invade my mind.

(End)

Maria Teresa

Somewhere within, there's a lesson to learn,
    And I hope you find it, yourself;
Maria Teresa, gave me a present,
    More precious than life itself.

Where does one begin, to tell of a sin,
    That never quite did take place;
Although it still burns, the memory remains,
    Of this girl with a smiling face.

She had just turned nineteen,
        and was of Spanish blood,
    Her hair was as black as coal;
Yet, when I looked, into her warm brown eyes,
    I could see right through to her soul.

"We met last year, before you were wed",
    She said to me with a smile;
"And now you know, what I knew then,
    It could only last a short while".

"For the woman you'd chosen,
        and I knew her quite well,
    Never had a good heart;
And though I feel guilty, for not telling you then,
    I knew, someday soon, you would part".

(1 of 4)

(2)

"Only a very few, let real tenderness shine through".
　　She spoke of me, in a soft tone;
"And if you'll take a chance, on real romance,
　　Maria would like to take you home".

How this young girl, whom I had hardly known,
　　Knew so much of my anguish and pain;
That as she moved closer, I imagined for a kiss,
　　From my eyes it began to rain.

She kissed me then, with the deepest passion I'd known,
　　Such heat within her lips;
That all I could do, while she lingered there,
　　Was place my hands on her hips.

"Only a very few, let real tenderness shine through"…
　　She said, as she looked into my eyes;
"The rest of the world, seem to just come and go,
　　And they disguise it with their lies".

"So, think it over and give me a call,
　　Tomorrow night about eight";
Then she turned and walked away,
　　Heading towards her fate.

(2 of 4)

(3)

The rest of that night, I tossed and turned,
    For some reason, I just couldn't sleep;
"Only a very few, let real tenderness shine through",
    Echoed the words, she did speak.

As I saw through the night, her beautiful eyes,
    And the tenderness she had shown;
That this lovely girl, with the warm brown eyes,
    Gave me kindness, I had never known.

All the next day, I felt good inside,
    A peace I had seldom known;
I vowed that, that night, I would call at eight,
    To nurture the seeds, she has sown.

With shock inside, I listened in quiet,
    As her aunt answered at eight;
Late that afternoon, in a stroke of doom,
    Maria Teresa had met her fate.

As if a last gesture, she had taken thirteen children,
    On a picnic, to the park;
An accident coming home, hurt none of the kids,
    Except Maria, she died just before dark.

(3 of 4)

(4)

So, if someone is truly tender towards you,
  This is someone, you should treat right;
Remember Maria Teresa, and the words that she lived,
  And don't let them get out of your sight.

For, "Only a very few, let real tenderness shine through."
  About myself, she had shared,
Or did she unlock, what was always inside me,
  Because, she really cared.

Whenever I see, a kind soul such as your's,
  In her memory, a vow I renew;
So, look in my eyes, straight on down to my soul, and…
  "Welcome to the very few."

(End)

The Little Cup

Each of us is born, with our own little cup,

    We must carry with us throughout life;

Friends try to fill it, with kindness and love,

    While others try to pour in some strife.

Mine is seldom empty, yet never quite full,

    With friends I would always share;

And as the years passed, the more that I gave,

    The more I had remaining there.

So drink from my cup, for tenderness breeds,

    It has nothing to do with good luck;

And when you are quenched, I hope you'll agree,

    Someone added more to your cup.

(End)

Sharing

For many past years, I've watched over you,
Protecting you, as best as I could;
I've seen you grow into a fine young woman,
Full of life and fun and good.

Helping you get through, some terrible times,
To me, was a simple pleasure;
I'm glad that I had, for you can still smile,
And to me, that's a real treasure.

We have always known, that we think so alike,
Sometimes it seems so ironic;
And after all these years, we enjoy each other more,
Caring seems great, when it's chronic.

If we had been strangers, and met recently,
And saw in the eyes of each other;
The mirrored image of someone, just like us,
By now, I am sure, we'd be lovers.

Something inside, seems to whisper to us,
We can hear it when we kiss;
"Consummating the love, we have for one another,
This is the sharing we miss".

(End)

<u>Sammy The Bee</u>

I have flown from flower to flower,
  On my search for pollen, you see;
I've spent all of my time, just buzzing around,
  Doing things for others, not for me.

I have checked out so many, many flowers,
  Nibbling at them all, so tenderly;
Caressing their petals, fulfilling their dreams,
  And again, there was nothing for me.

More hurriedly, I started out with the sun,
  And came home with the moon, you see;
I even tried life in the desolate meadows,
  Where flowers cried out, "Please help me".

Some of these flowers, are into "S" and "M",
  It's my stinger they wanted, not me;
And I never was one, to stay where not wanted,
  Believing I was born to be free.

At last, I have found, the most perfect flower,
  All I could want it to be;
The nectar there, makes the sweetest honey,
  And that flower is what you are to me.

(End)

Sharon's Jungle

All fuzzy and warm, and cute as could be,
  Like a koala bear, you are to me;
Yet one day you fell, from an overhanging tree,
  Into life's jungle, you see.

Therein, all sorts of predators reside,
  Some are as beautiful as can be;
Some just attack with such brutal force,
  They offer so little time to flee.

First there was Bobby, with the crocodile eyes,
  And Dave with the cobra's mouth;
Down a deep ravine, lived Ray the tiger,
  Who loved to play cat and mouse.

Then there was Dennis, the mute hyena,
  I don't think he knew how to laugh;
And then again Brian, the forgetful elephant,
  If he wounds you, you'd surely get staph.

(1 of 2)

(2)

Others are of a species, yet unknown,
　　Some deadly, you see at a glance;
For these are the kind, that seem so benign,
　　They stalk you, then try to en'trance.

You see, everyone goes through life's jungle,
　　And in your's, many carnivores might be;
But as you pass through, many friends are there too,
　　Maybe even a frog, such as me.

So, don't look down, for a little green friend on the ground,
　　To find me, I'll give you this hint;
For you're not a bear, and I'm not a frog,
　　But if you kiss me, I might be your prince.

(End)

A Sensitive Man

Looking back at the past, my life up 'til now,
    And remembering, as best as I can;
Has but one saving grace, from all the bittersweet,
    It has made me a sensitive man.

Someone who could never, quite like what I saw,
    In the mirror, as through life I ran;
Has found that by looking after the needs of others,
    Has transformed me into a sensitive man.

Mostly giving of my time, and sometimes a hand out,
    I embarked on my new found plan;
And occasionally an attentive ear,
        to someone with heartache,
    Would bring tears to this sensitive man.

If you should want, just someone to talk with,
    Know that I'm here and you can;
And if you need someone, to be kind and gentle,
    Remember, this sensitive man.

(End)

Cathy

This is a story, of a mother of three,
  Most recently, a pair of twins;
My niece invited her along, and we all went out dancing,
  And primarily, where my involvement begins.

She seemed so unhappy, it had been so long,
  Since she got out, and enjoyed herself;
She spoke with love and hate, of the father of her children,
  And a pain inside, that I've often felt.

As the evening went by, and we danced close together,
  I guess, I sensed all of her need;
To be cuddled and kissed, and loved more than ever,
  But most of all, treated tenderly.

After a few months, the reality had struck her,
  That she and the father, would never wed;
And I knew from experience, loves not like a faucet,
  You can't just turn it off, when it's dead.

During my life, I'd been with many a woman,
  Like a good book, I was well read;
Telling her it was not love, and knowing it was not pity,
  With mutual need, I invited her to my bed.

(1 of 2)

Now, on this point she agreed, but the day's time ran out,
    To tend to our needs, properly;
For a mother of three, has so little time to spend,
    So, we set a tentative date, for next week.

"Fail to plan, plan to fail", the words of some wise man,
    Was not going to happen, to me;
Waiting for something to happen, can get awfully lonely,
    Let me be the first, to tell you that, of spontaneity.

Let me say that I loved her, and just keep it simple,
    Forget the details, or the time, or the place;
Let's just say that she found out, I really know how,
    To just put a smile, on an unhappy lady's face.

I hope you can see, that I'm not being crass,
    It's mostly her friendship I need;
And if she should again, want to touch the stars,
    I'd help her out, gentlemanly.

You see, sometimes you love, because you're in love,
    And sometimes you love, just for need;
I guess I shared, for she's a lovely young woman,
    And I'm happy that she shared for me.

(End)

Poet

A gift of the pen, somehow adds power to the mind,
　　It can become, an awesome responsibility;
To determine what to write, when there's so much in life,
　　That's suppressed, and longs to be free.

And so, at last, I took up the noble task,
　　Of writing, what needs to be said;
Of things that are in danger, of becoming extinct,
　　So, the day would never come, when they're dead.

I don't write of food, and I don't write of money,
　　And I don't write of hatred and strife;
I speak of love, and truth, and honesty, and giving,
　　For these add real sustenance, to life.

I speak of man's spirit, incarnate,
　　Perpetuating all the good things, I've listed above;
And if you want, to put a tag on helping one's neighbor,
　　Why not use a catchy little word like "Love".

(End)

Day to Day

I know that by now, you know how I feel,
    And I know that you know, that it's true;
And if patience is a virtue, then I am a saint,
    So why is it, I always feel blue?

I've poured out my heart to you, turned my soul inside out,
    And somewhere along the way, touched a nerve;
But to satisfy the craving, somewhere deep down inside of me,
    It seems our kisses and embraces, never serve.

If there's one thing that I despise, it's walking on this fence,
    Never demanding, but always wanting more;
So, I put the question to you now, to save my sanity,
    Shall we love, or should I head for the door?

You know the chance we take, of destroying all we've built,
    All the trust, all the caring, all the honesty;
But I'd just like to point out, these are also building blocks,
    For some, a month; for some, a year; for some, eternity.

I'm sorry to put you on the spot, yet I really need your answer,
    For you see, I can not go on much longer this way;
And I can not promise you, that it will last forever,
    The best we can expect from life, is day to day.

(End)

Rag Doll

Tossed into this closet,

    When you were near fifteen;

And I was still, so full of life,

    My button eyes did glean.

Left to all the dust,

    My patch-work started to fade;

My hair of rug, is under someone's shoes,

    Dear God, why was I made?

Sitting in this darkness,

    Waiting so patiently;

My stitched-up mouth, can not cry out,

    Won't someone set me free?

(End)

Rooster

Call it a pub, or a gilded cage,
　　But it's just an old barn, to me;
And in this place, you'll find the hens,
　　Dispense brew, and a bit of feed.

Now, I'm just a tired old rooster,
　　And somewheres 'round about nine;
I start moseying on down to the barn,
　　And have me a good old time.

The place is patrolled, by junk-yard dogs,
　　And what really doesn't make sense;
They roam through the barn, ejecting troublesome roosters,
　　And they try to do it without "a fence".

Although the place packs, with roosters and chickens,
　　You'll occasionally find a cow, and some "bull";
And when they're not busy, doin' the barnyard strut,
　　They're busy, trying to keep their troughs full.

I don't like to be teased with McNuggets,
　　So I bring my own chicken with me;
But if you really are tired, of Colonel Sanders,
　　Come to the barn, where a chicken can be free.

(End)

The Last Flower

I once had some flower seeds,
    And I placed them in rich soil;
I watered them and fed them well,
    For they were not much toil.

When they began to blossom,
    I offered them to everyone I knew;
Those who accepted are happy now,
    And all I had left were two.

Giving one of these to a young woman,
    She grasped at it without a look;
As though she could save beauty for a rainy day,
    She squashed it within a book.

Seeing what had happened to that flower,
    I'm hesitant to offer the last of the two;
But if there's anyone who appreciates real beauty,
    I have one flower remaining, and it's for you.

(End)

Uncle Teddy

Your Teddy bear is dead,
   Don't look so surprised;
He died of a broken heart,
   And he had tears in his eyes.

Your Teddy bear is dead,
   He was hurt by someone close;
And as you well know,
   That's when it hurts the most.

Your Teddy bear is dead,
   Although he tried so hard;
To find little ways to please you,
   It only got him scarred.

Your Teddy bear is dead,
   Of this you can be sure;
What bear can survive,
   Without hugs anymore?

Your Teddy bear is dead,
   And no one really knows why;
He wished to send a last message,
   And the message is "Goodbye".

(End)

The Mosaic

Endeavoring to build, such a great foundation,
  They set-out to do their task;
A custom-fitted, mosaic work-of-art,
  Something beautiful, that would really last.

He had a multitude, of magnificent plans,
  And carried them around, in his head;
Desiring that each block, fit together perfectly,
  Before the day, they would be laid.

She said that sounds good, and was ever so helpful,
  Adding the exact amount of cement;
Forming the blocks, in such shapes of unusual beauty,
  With diligence, that did not relent.

It was very important, that this foundation be strong,
  And therefore, substantially thick;
For it was to support, a home for their family,
  A shelter, made of fine stone and brick.

(1 of 3)

(2)

To the man with his plans, it became a labor of love,
    And he named each piece, correspondingly;
On some bricks you could read "tenderness",
        and some would read "caring",
    And others; "respect and sincerity".

She loved as she read them, the meaning of
        "tenderness", and of "caring",
    Which stood out boldly on the brick;
And so, she added a "kiss", and a "hug",
    Even a "glance", seemed to click.

After a month, they had piles of bricks,
    Named "sincerity", "tenderness", "respect", and "caring";
And they had even larger piles, of "kiss"(s), and "hug"(s),
    With some "glance"(s), and recently added "sharing".

And then it seems, she lost sight of his dreams,
    She said, "I'm not ready for this";
Whether it was the man himself, or whether his plans,
    She told him right after he gave her a "kiss".

(2 of 3)

(3)

Now he just sits, in a pile of rubble,

    Of what once were such beautiful bricks;

And remembers the moment, that each of them were made,

    Finding it difficult, not to feel sick.

Fashioning one more brick, just by himself,

    To keep busy and help him cope;

Praying that someday soon, she will be ready,

    He inscribes on this one, the word "hope".

As he gets up, and starts to walk away,

    He looks back, wondering if there is a chance;

That they will ever finish, his work of love,

    Then, he sees "hope" next to "glance".

He had worked so hard, this last month of Spring,

    In a few days it is Summer, then comes Fall;

And although he will miss her love,

      especially at this time of year,

    Come this Autumn, he will start building a wall.

(End)

<u>Ellie's Story</u>

I listened to this waitress,
  With friends, she had a chat;
Talking of another place,
  Where she had eaten at.

The food there wasn't spectacular,
  Breakfast seldom seems to be;
And the service was less than average,
  Many of their patrons would agree.

For all they served, at little cost,
  The price was really great;
And although it seems cruel to say it,
  That's all that made the place rate.

After her meal, and sitting back,
  From taking all her fill;
That's when Ellie finally discovered,
  The restaurant's surprise thrill.

(1 of 2)

(2)

At precisely the time, she'd enjoy her coffee,
    With just a teaspoon of cream;
This ugly little guy, stopped for a visit,
    I'll bet she wanted to scream.

He stared-up to look her in the face,
    As she could plainly see;
This good-sized roach, with antennae moving,
    While perched upon her knee.

So, if you plan on dining out,
    Or just a coffee or tea;
It pays to check out where you go,
    Remember Ellie's knee.

(End)

Tuesdays

If … "Mondays" are truly "Blue"…,

    Then Tuesdays must be brown;

For it seems, on this particular day,

    All of the world tries to beat you down.

They did not see the mountainous Monday workload,

    And that you had done better than your best;

All they can see is the little bit remaining,

    While demanding that you finish the rest.

So, I give you a little secret to happiness,

    In order to keep your spirit aloft;

Smile at them, agree and always say yes,

    Inwardly remembering, on Tuesdays,

        yes means "f_ _k off".

(End)

"Honey Child"

Youngsters think the world is their's,
    To grab, or to pick and choose;
But the truth is, the mature adult,
    Is doing a lot more than taking a snooze.

We have an advantage of some wisdom,
    Maybe, from having made a mistake;
Although we've gained knowledge, money or power,
    Our best effort is in caring for our mate.

Whether it be with good friends or neighbors,
    Our word is as good as gold;
And if this were the only by-product,
    I don't mind so much, growing old.

So, Honey Child, I tell you now,
    I'm looking for a mate;
And though I have some patience,
    I really don't want to wait.

A younger man would promise you, the world,
    The skin of the truth, stuffed with lies;
While I, Honey Child, would anticipate your needs,
    And, if in my power, everyday would be a surprise.

(End)

"Shabby"

Cold was my place,
  Cold filled my space;
Time in my haste,
  Time was my waste.

Then came a trace,
  Then came your face;
Love filled my space,
  Love I could taste.

Ice did retrace,
  Ice from my base;
Now, in my case,
  Now, Love did replace.

Like flowers sunning in a vase,
  Like warmth from your embrace;
Dear woman with lace,
  Dearest woman of grace.

You melt me!!

(End)

About the Author

"Sam" (George J) Barder, was born in 1944, and served in the United States Air Force for over ten years as an enlisted man, and served as a nuclear missile launch officer during the 1960's. Since then he has looked at life differently, and expresses it within his poems. He had a rich life doing many different things after leaving the service. He is now retired and still serves his community as a minister in the Universal Life Church.

Over the many years and many experiences of life, he has been inspired to write this collection of poems, that he hopes you will enjoy.

He can be reached with your comments by email, and would enjoy hearing from you.

samgjbee0@gmail.com

Copies of this book are available on
Amazon.com
and Kindle e-book

Made in the USA
Middletown, DE
27 August 2023

37260335R00021